KNIGHTS OF RIGHT

Also by M'Lin Rowley

Knights of Right, book 2: *The Silver Coat*

Illustrations by Michael Walton

Visit us at ShadowMountain.com

Library of Congress Cataloging-in-Publication Data
Rowley, M'Lin.
    The falcon shield / M'Lin Rowley.
        p.   cm. — (Knights of right ; bk. 1)
    Audience: 4–6.
    Summary: While exploring the woods behind their house, brothers
Joseph, twelve, and Ben, ten, discover the castle of King Arthur, who
has traveled through time to train them as modern-day knights of the
Round Table, sending them on a quest against a real-life enemy.
    ISBN 978-1-60641-103-2 (paperbound)
    [1. Knights and knighthood—Fiction.   2. Conduct of life—Fiction.
3. Drug abuse—Fiction.   4. Brothers—Fiction.   5. Arthur, King—Fiction.   6. Kings,
queens, rulers, etc.—Fiction.]   I. Title.
    PZ7.R79834Fal 2009
    [Fic]—dc22
                                                                          2009003593

Printed in the United States of America
Malloy Lithographing Incorporated, Ann Arbor, MI

10   9   8   7   6   5   4   3   2   1

KNIGHTS OF RIGHT

BOOK 1
THE FALCON SHIELD

M'LIN ROWLEY

SHADOW
MOUNTAIN

1

THE BLACK KNIGHT

Ten-year-old Ben excitedly climbed the fence in his backyard. He turned around to see if his twelve-year-old brother, Joseph, was following him. They had lived in their new house a whole month and they still hadn't explored the woods behind it. Mom and Dad were on vacation, and Samantha was their babysitter. Sam was pretty cool for an eighteen-year-old girl. She had known Joseph and Ben forever, because she was the daughter of their parents' best friends. At the moment, she was busy playing games with their little sister, Katie. Sam thought the boys were in the tree house. It was a perfect time to check things out.

"I don't think this is a good idea, Ben. We probably shouldn't be out here," Joseph whispered, glancing around nervously at the huge trees. Ben smiled to reassure his older brother and ran off into the woods, motioning for Joseph to follow. They soon found a squirrel to chase, and Joseph forgot to be worried.

They chased the squirrel into a hollow log. Ben stood at one end while Joseph stood at the other, hoping they could catch it when it came out again.

"I told you that you would like it out here," Ben said, but Joseph wasn't listening.

He was staring at something behind Ben, and his jaw dropped. He pointed and began stammering. Slowly, Ben turned around to see what Joseph was looking at.

Standing between two trees about fifty feet away was a large man in shiny black armor. He looked like something straight out of a history book—a really scary history book. The sun glinted off the knight's helmet, and Ben had to shield his eyes.

"Okay, that's . . . weird. M-maybe he's some guy getting ready for Halloween," Ben suggested in a shaky voice.

"Getting ready for Halloween in August?" Joseph squeaked. "I think we should run." As the knight raised a slick, black crossbow loaded with a very real-looking arrow, Ben agreed. In a panic, both boys took off running, forgetting which way they had come. Ben stumbled and almost fell as an arrow struck a tree right above his head.

"He's really shooting at us!" Ben yelled, looking up at the arrow above him in the tree.

"This way!" Joseph cried, running to the right.

For once Ben didn't complain about being bossed around. The whole forest seemed against them as they tried to get away. Roots reached up to trip them, branches blocked their path, and the sun shone hotter and hotter as they ran. Soon they couldn't see the knight behind them. Finally, Ben had to stop to catch his breath. "Hold up, Joseph. I can't run anymore."

Joseph stopped and stood panting by his brother.

"If I'm sweating this bad, imagine how stinky that guy is in full armor." Ben laughed nervously at his own joke as he stared into the trees behind them. He couldn't see or hear any sign of the knight. Maybe they had just imagined it.

"Do you think we lost him?" Joseph asked hopefully.

Just then the Black Knight stepped out from behind a tree. He was closer than he had been when they'd first seen him.

Frightened, the boys ducked behind a huge fallen log. "You'd think that armor would slow him down a little," Ben gasped.

Joseph pointed at something in the

distance. It looked like a stone wall, but they couldn't see much of it through the trees.

"Let's head for that wall and see if we can find somewhere to hide," Joseph whispered nervously. They crept slowly away from the knight, making sure he couldn't see them. When they thought they were far enough away, they ran quickly toward the wall.

The two boys had almost reached it when they skidded to a stop before a wide stream. Up close they could see that the wall was actually part of a crumbling old castle. First a knight in armor, then an old castle. What kind of forest was this?

"Hey! This is the moat for that castle!" Ben motioned toward the still water that circled the wall. "Do you think there are alligators in it, or could we swim across it to get away?"

Joseph pointed across the water. A drawbridge was lowering not far from where they stood.

"What do you think?" Joseph asked.

"This could be the Black Knight's castle, and we're running straight into his trap!"

An arrow whistled into the ground at Joseph's feet. "We don't have a choice. The knight's shooting at us out here. Let's get in there!" They raced across the drawbridge. On the other side, Joseph found the crank, and both boys pulled with all their might to turn the handle and raise the drawbridge again. Ben caught sight of the knight's black helmet and his fist raised in anger as the drawbridge closed.

The courtyard looked deserted, but then, across the square, the large doors of the castle began to creak open.

2

INSIDE THE CASTLE

"Did Mom and Dad tell you we were moving near a haunted castle?" Ben asked as they stood, watching the doors open.

"No," Joseph answered. "And they didn't tell me our new neighbor was a crazy killer knight."

Before Ben could reply, they heard someone calling to them from inside the castle. "Welcome, welcome, my friends! Come in, come in. I've been hoping you'd come!"

Ben and Joseph looked at each other in

surprise. The voice sounded friendly. They walked toward the door. As they entered the castle, they could see an old man sitting on a throne at the end of a long room.

"Yes, come closer now," the man motioned, still smiling. A crown sat gently on his head, and his dark red cloak just touched the floor. A sleek hunting dog slept by his feet.

"Wow," Joseph whispered in awe. "He looks like King Arthur in that book at the library."

"If you say so," Ben whispered back, shrugging his shoulders. "He doesn't look anything like the King Arthur in the movie."

"I'm sorry to disappoint you," the king laughed. "My name really is Arthur, although

I don't know anything about—what did you call it—a movie?"

"Oh, sorry," Ben stammered. Joseph elbowed his brother, and together they bowed as low as they could without tipping over.

"I have been expecting you, young Joseph and Benjamin," the king continued, as the boys raised their heads in disbelief. "But shouldn't there be another? A girl?"

Ben looked at Joseph and shrugged. Ben thought what Katie's reaction might be to the Black Knight. She wouldn't be scared. She'd want to get close to him with a stick so she could scratch his black armor to see if there were rainbow colors underneath. She did that to anything black ever since Mom bought her that special scratch-off art-paper stuff. The Black Knight would love that!

So how did King Arthur know about his family—and what was an old guy from medieval times doing here? Joseph wondered.

"A girl with us? If you mean my sister, Katie, well, she's barely three. I don't think it would be a good idea to bring her here," Joseph answered hurriedly.

"Well," King Arthur said, "I may be wrong. Please, allow me to explain why you are here. You have been chosen as knights in training for the Round Table. Your task as knights, if you choose to accept it, is to fight against evil and stand for truth. It is a hard task but very rewarding." Arthur looked at them as calmly as if he were telling the time.

Joseph's eyes widened and Ben's jaw dropped. "Us? You want us? We're just kids!" Joseph gasped.

"Children you may be, but you are noble and brave. I do not believe that age prevents anyone from choosing right," King Arthur assured them.

"Cool. I accept!" Ben said excitedly. The king smiled and then looked to Joseph for his answer.

Joseph shook his head to clear it. "Um, King Arthur, sir, Your Majesty, or whatever we should call you, I don't get it. Did we travel back in time or something? I mean, you lived a long time ago, and no offense, but there aren't kings and castles and knights that fight evil anymore."

"Ah, but that is where you are wrong, young Joseph. If ever there was a need for knights, that time is now. And to answer your question, you have not traveled back in time. I am the one who has traveled forward to find you."

"Well, okay, we'll be glad to help you," Joseph said. "But it can't take too long. We have to get home. Sam's probably looking for us by now."

"Wonderful! But there is one thing you must learn before you can begin. Before you can become knights, you must first protect yourselves against the enemy."

"How do we do that?" Ben asked, picturing himself coming out of the castle with an awesome secret weapon to face the Black Knight.

"I was hoping you'd ask." King Arthur smiled. "Come sit here in front of me, and I'll tell you a story."

Joseph quickly sat down next to King Arthur's hunting dog and petted it. The dog nuzzled closer to him. Ben sat down too, disappointed that they were hearing a story instead of getting a cool weapon.

The king leaned forward, and his eyes sparkled with excitement as he began his tale.

3

THE TWO-HEADED SNAKE

"In my kingdom there was once a terrible knight, who was feared by all." As King Arthur began his story, Ben perked up.

"We saw him!" Ben said excitedly.

"Be quiet, Ben!" Joseph whispered. "Stop interrupting."

"I was only going to say that one little thing," Ben grumbled.

"You saw the Black Knight, Ben. He is evil, yes, but this knight was twice as coldhearted and ruthless. He was called the Two-Headed

Snake because he carried two swords and fought with them both at once. He was so skilled and quick that no opponent had a chance. Not one knight ever hit the Two-Headed Snake with a sword stroke of his own," King Arthur continued. "Many of my noblest and best knights were brought down trying to protect my people from his cruelty. All the living knights gathered at the Round Table to discuss what could be done.

"As we talked, a young boy about your age crawled out from under the Round Table where he had been hiding. He stood before all the knights and claimed he could defeat the Two-Headed Snake. Every knight laughed at him. But I sensed his pure heart and I agreed to let him face the knight, even though everyone

in the kingdom thought I was mad, sending an innocent boy to his death."

"Did he make it?" Ben asked worriedly.

King Arthur smiled and held up his hand. "If you let me continue, I will tell you," Arthur laughed. "The boy approached the Two-Headed Snake. While he was still a good distance away, far from the range of the evil knight's swords, he shot a small poisoned dart with a blowgun. The dart struck the knight through a small flaw in his armor. The Two-Headed Snake fell dead. Even two deadly swords could not stop a tiny dart. Peace was restored."

The king finished and sat back, looking at them expectantly. Joseph continued to pet the dog thoughtfully as he considered the story.

"That is so cool!" Ben declared. "When do I get a blowgun and some poisoned darts?"

4

HEART OF A FALCON

King Arthur chuckled softly. "I am sorry, young Benjamin. You have to earn any weapons you receive. But there is a different lesson that I want you to learn from this story. It is a lesson the Two-Headed Snake never learned."

"Does it have something to do with protecting ourselves from the enemy?" Joseph asked as the dog next to him snuffled quietly in its sleep.

"Yes, it does. Remember this story as you

complete your first quest. When you have successfully defeated your first enemy, you may come and see me again."

King Arthur whistled. The dog's head perked up as a beautiful falcon flew in through an open window, carrying two long leather gloves in its talons. The falcon dropped the gloves in the king's lap and landed on his arm.

"This is True Heart. He will help you prepare for the enemy you will face. Watch for his clues. The first step in defeating an enemy is to know who or what your enemy is. True Heart is a brave bird and has served me well. Take good care of him for me." King Arthur stroked True Heart's head and then handed

one glove to Joseph. "This glove will protect your arm from his claws."

As soon as Joseph put on the glove, True Heart fluttered over to his arm. The king handed the second glove to Ben.

"We get a falcon? No way!" Ben said with excitement.

"Yes," King Arthur said. "It is . . . how did you say it, Benjamin? So cold?" The boys started laughing at Arthur's mistake.

"You mean *so cool*, Your Majesty." The king laughed with them.

"Now, boys, it is time for you to return to your home. I sense the Black Knight has left the woods for now. You will be safe if you hurry. Good luck on your quest, my friends," Arthur said as Ben and Joseph stood up. "I believe in you. I know you will do well."

"Don't worry, we won't let you down!" Joseph called back as he and Ben left.

Together they let down the drawbridge. Then they slowly crept across it, watching the trees on the other side for any sign of the Black Knight. When they were halfway across, they heard the castle doors closing behind them.

It doesn't matter, Ben told himself. An old guy like Arthur wouldn't be able to help them if the Black Knight appeared anyway. Joseph felt a little better with the falcon on his arm.

Once they crossed the drawbridge, they ran to the nearest fallen tree and crouched down. After several long moments of silence, Joseph raised his head above the log and scanned the woods around them. When he signaled that everything was clear, they crept to the next tree and waited. Then they sneaked to the next tree. The Black Knight never appeared.

"Sam will kill us if she finds out we were out here," Joseph winced. "With all this spy stuff, ducking and hiding, it will take forever to get home. Let's just run for it."

"Can you lead us home, T. H.?" Ben asked the falcon.

"T. H.?" Joseph asked.

"True Heart is a nice name and all, but it's too long. I thought T. H. could be our nick-name for him," Ben said.

True Heart took off and flew slowly above the trees, circling and waiting for the boys to catch up. They made it to their back fence and started to climb.

Sam was standing on the back porch, hands on her hips. "You guys are so dead," she in-formed them. "And what's up with the bird?"

5

TRUE HEART'S
FIRST CLUE

"We're really sorry we went into the woods without telling you, Sam. Can't we have cookies now?" Ben begged.

Dinner was over, and they were still sitting around the table. Sam had believed Joseph when he told her they found the falcon in the woods. She even let them bring True Heart into the house. All she said was that the falcon was clearly tame and they should put up flyers to try to find its owner. The boys didn't argue with her, mostly because they were too busy eating dinner.

Their current problem was that Sam was still mad they'd taken off into the woods without telling her. She and Katie were enjoying the cookies she had made, and Ben and Joseph were practically drooling.

"Birdie want cookie?" Katie asked while holding up a piece of cookie towards True Heart, who stood on Ben's arm. The falcon climbed off Ben's arm carefully onto the table and then hopped over to Katie. He nibbled at the cookie, making Katie giggle. After the cookie was gone, True Heart ran his beak through Katie's curly hair, trying to get her to feed him again and making her giggle even more.

"Don't spoil him, Katie. He's a fighting falcon and shouldn't get fat," Joseph sighed.

"I'm going to go put Katie in the tub. You guys stay out of trouble." Sam pointed two fingers to her eyes and then at them. "I'm watching you!" She picked up Katie and went upstairs.

"Ooh, scary, she's watching us," Ben snickered. Joseph smiled, too. True Heart launched off the table and flew out an open window.

"Hey, T. H., come back!" Joseph called after the bird. Both boys frowned. King Arthur wouldn't be happy if his special falcon disappeared the very first day. But a few minutes later, True Heart flew back in with a piece of paper gripped tightly in his talons.

"What's this?" Joseph asked. The paper fluttered to the table. It had a skull and crossbones painted in the middle.

"It's one of the clues that King Arthur was talking about!" Ben exclaimed. "The one that will help us figure out what our quest is!" Joseph and Ben stared at the paper, trying to understand what it meant.

"Pirates," Ben stated seriously. "We get to fight pirates."

Joseph laughed so hard he fell off his chair and rolled on the ground.

"King Arthur wouldn't send us to fight pi-rates!" Joseph said.

"You come up with an idea, then," Ben said, shoving Joseph as he got to his feet.

"Hey!" Joseph barked back, throwing a

punch at Ben. Pretty soon they were rolling around on the ground fighting.

"Whoa! Back off, guys! It's bedtime!" Sam rushed in, having to yell to be heard over their hollering. Once she'd separated them, she spoke quietly.

"You guys are acting so weird today. Something's going on, and trust me, I'm going to find out what it is. Upstairs, both of you." She pointed to their bedrooms. Ben stuffed the clue into his pocket and started for the stairs.

"Wait," Joseph said, "we need to find somewhere for T. H. to sleep."

Sam looked around thoughtfully. "I'll put him in the shed tonight, but you'd better have a good explanation for your parents when they get home."

They nodded and ran up to bed before Sam could change her mind or ask them any more questions.

6

CLUELESS

Joseph woke with a start the next morning when something soft but heavy dropped on his face. He groaned and held it up to see what it was. A little black vinyl bag filled with colorful plastic doctor's tools—Katie's toy doctor kit. True Heart landed on his alarm clock. It was late in the morning, and the sun poured in through the open window.

Katie stomped into Joseph's room. "That's mine, T. T.!" She shook her finger angrily at the bird.

"His name is T. H., not T. T.," Joseph said, sitting up. "And he was giving me this for a clue, I think."

"Clues, T. T.? Why my doctor toy clues?" she asked the bird, trotting up to pet its back.

"I don't know yet. Maybe Ben will." Joseph rolled out of bed to go get Ben. He shook his snoring brother until Ben woke up.

"Go away!" Ben waved his hand sleepily, trying to slap Joseph out of the way.

"T. H. gave us another clue," Joseph explained.

Suddenly Ben was wide awake. "What is it?" he asked, sitting up in bed quickly.

"Katie's doctor kit is the clue." Joseph held up the little bag.

"The doctor's office is evil. That must be

the quest. We have to stay far away from the doctor's office," Ben guessed.

"But what does the skull and crossbones have to do with a doctor's office?"

"Duh! You can die in the hospital or a doctor's office," Ben said.

Joseph laughed. "I don't think that's our quest. The clue must mean something else. The doctor isn't the enemy." This quest thing

was going to be harder than they had expected.

Sam was cooking breakfast when the boys went downstairs. Their parents would be back the next day. Joseph missed his parents, but he was glad they didn't have to explain everything just yet. Sam said she'd let T.H. out of the shed that morning, and she was working on a flyer about a tame falcon. Joseph didn't think it could hurt because he didn't think King Arthur would see the flyer.

After breakfast, Joseph and Ben headed outside to play baseball. They hadn't been outside for very long when True Heart flew down with a small, strange looking leafy branch in his beak.

"What's up? Is this another clue?" Ben

asked True Heart. But when Ben reached for it, the falcon wouldn't let go. True Heart shook his head back and forth excitedly with his beak clamped down tightly on the plant.

"What is wrong, T. H.? Why can't we have the clue?" Joseph asked. Just then Sam came out of the house holding the phone for Ben.

Ben took the phone, listened for a second, and then gave an excited yes. When he handed the phone back to Sam, he was grinning from ear to ear.

"That was Duke! He invited me over to his house. Wow! This is a first! The new kid on the block, and already I get to hang out with the cool kids! I guess you'll just have to play with Katie, Joseph," Ben teased.

"We still have to solve the clues!" Joseph complained.

"We can do that later," Ben said as he grabbed his bike and headed down the street. He was so excited he didn't see True Heart circling in the air above him.

7

BEN'S BATTLE

As soon as Ben arrived, Duke led his friends to the garage. Once they were inside Duke whispered to Ben, "We figured you haven't been here long enough to know what's cool, so we decided to teach you."

Ben was confused. "What do you mean? It's hot in here. Let's go ride bikes or something," he suggested. But Duke ignored him and tossed a can of spray paint to each boy. "What's this for?" Ben asked.

"You inhale the fumes, stupid. It's what all

the cool kids are doing to get high," Duke explained impatiently.

Ben's eyes widened. "That's not fun. I think we should just play some basketball," he suggested.

"This guy's a loser," one of the boys snorted. The others agreed.

"We should warn the rest of the world," Duke said, shaking his can of spray paint. "Grab him. We'll paint 'loser' all over his sissy shirt."

Matt grabbed his shoulders, and Todd caught hold of one arm. Ben raised his other arm to protect his face just as True Heart screeched loudly from somewhere outside. Duke pressed his finger down, and paint sprayed out of the can in a steady stream.

Suddenly there was a loud snapping noise. Ben opened his eyes and was astonished to find a shield strapped to his arm. The paint hit the shield and splattered everywhere.

Duke had a strange look on his face.

"What the—what's going on?" Duke dropped the can and waved his hand in the air in front of him. He seemed to be trying to figure out why no paint had hit Ben. Ben tried to keep from laughing when he realized Duke couldn't see or feel the shield.

"This kid is creepy—let's get out of here!" Duke said. The boys scattered, leaving Ben standing in Duke's garage with spray cans and paint splatters around his feet.

Ben took the shield off his arm to look at it more closely. To his surprise, none of the paint had stuck to the shield. The metal was shiny and new. On the front was the image of a falcon with a snake in its claws and an olive branch in its mouth. As he examined the shield, True Heart flew in through an open door and landed on his shoulder.

"Hey, T. H.! You look great on this shield! So this is what you were trying to warn me about. I guess I need to find some different friends."

Ben rode home slowly, balancing the shield on his handlebars. He couldn't wait to find out if Joseph could see it too.

8

JOSEPH'S TEST

"Your shield is awesome, Ben! I wish I had one." Joseph sighed as they looked at the shield together in the tree house.

"When do you think we'll face a real enemy?" Ben said.

"I don't know," said Joseph. "What could Duke and your shield have to do with T. H.'s clues and the dart in King Arthur's story? We'll have to talk about it later, though, because Dad is waiting for me. Take good care of T. H., okay? And don't go back to the castle without me."

Mom and Dad had returned home a few hours before, and now Dad had to go back to their old house to finish up some repairs before the new owners moved in. Joseph was going with him to have one last backyard campout with his friends from the old neighborhood.

"Do you have your sleeping bag?" Dad called from the house.

"Yeah, Dad," Joseph called back as he started climbing down the ladder.

"Then let's get the show on the road. It's camping time!" A few hours later they were parked in front of Joseph's friend Parker's house.

"Well, have a good time! Remember who

you are and where you live," Dad joked. "I'll pick you up in the morning."

"Sounds great! I'll see you tomorrow, Dad!" Joseph hopped out of the car and ran up the front steps with his sleeping bag and his backpack.

"Hello, Joseph! Just head out back," Parker's mom greeted him cheerfully. The tent was already set up, and the gang was sitting inside playing Uno® and eating pizza. He didn't recognize one of the boys, but the rest were Joseph's good friends. He knew they were going to have a blast tonight.

"Joseph!" They all cheered and made room for him in the game. The evening passed quickly.

As the sun went down, the boys began to

talk about what to do next. David thought they should go doorbell-ditching. Parker said he'd stashed some rolls of toilet paper in the shed so they could toilet-paper Jenni Ward's house.

"Why don't we just keep playing Uno®?" Joseph asked. Then a brilliant light lit up the tent, followed closely by thunder. Soon a little rain started tapping on the fabric of the tent.

"I guess doorbell-ditching and toilet-papering are out," Parker said. He set up a lantern in the middle of the sleeping bags. The new boy, Jason, pulled something out of his pocket.

"Here, try one of these. We'll get so hyper—it's crazy!" He laughed and tossed a little orange container to one of the boys after popping a pill in his mouth.

"What are they?" Joseph asked, hoping the boy would say it was some kind of candy.

"They're my mom's prescription pills. She doesn't even know I have them!" Jason laughed proudly.

Joseph felt butterflies in his stomach. He knew he shouldn't take pills if he wasn't sick.

"I don't think that's a good idea," Joseph mumbled.

"It's okay, Joseph. We tried them before. Nothing happened," Parker said quietly.

Joseph shook his head. "I'm not doing that."

"Then go home," the new boy said. Joseph glanced at his friends in surprise.

"Do you think you're too good for us now or something?" David asked.

Everyone seemed embarrassed, but no one stood up for Joseph.

"Better run home to your mommy, Joseph," Jason said.

"We don't need a party pooper here," Parker mumbled.

"Fine. I'll go home," Joseph snapped. He gathered his stuff, unzipped the tent, and stepped outside into the drizzling cold rain.

The back door of Parker's house was locked. Joseph didn't want to knock, and he wasn't going back into the tent. He put his sleeping bag on the back porch and curled down in the bottom of it. He hoped he wouldn't get too wet.

Joseph was almost asleep when he heard a loud snap. He was too tired to stick his head out of the sleeping bag to see what it was. *Maybe the tent fell down on my stupid friends,* he thought hopefully.

The next morning when Joseph woke up it was still raining, but he wasn't wet. Resting above him was a huge shield that had covered him perfectly and protected him from the rain. His shield looked just like Ben's. It had a falcon on the front with a snake in its claws and an olive branch in its mouth.

Just then Parker's mom opened the back door. She was carrying a tray full of breakfast.

"Joseph! What are you doing out here? Why aren't you in the tent?" she asked.

Joseph nervously explained what had happened and asked if he could call his dad.

A short time later, his dad drove up. He helped Joseph carry his camping gear out to the car. He didn't say anything about the shield, so Joseph guessed that he couldn't see it. Joseph just slipped it on top of his gear in the trunk while his dad talked to Parker's mom.

After his dad had finished talking, they drove away.

"Joseph, I'm really proud of your decision," his dad said. "I don't think you got any breakfast, did you?"

Joseph felt good inside, but he was hungry. "No, I didn't," he said.

"Well, why don't we stop somewhere special on the way home, then? Are you okay with that?"

Joseph grinned. "I sure am!" He couldn't wait to get home and show Ben the shield he'd earned. He'd hang it next to Ben's in the tree house until they could get away to see King Arthur again.

9

PROTECTED FROM
THE ENEMY

Joseph and Ben ran through the woods as True Heart led them back to King Arthur's castle. The boys kept waiting for an arrow to appear out of nowhere, but the woods were quiet. Maybe the Black Knight didn't always know when they entered the forest.

Joseph was sure True Heart would warn them if he sensed any danger, and even though they kept an eye out themselves, they never caught a glimpse of black through the trees. When they reached the castle, the drawbridge was down. King Arthur was waiting for them in the throne room, just like before.

"We did it, Your Majesty! We got our shields!" Joseph called excitedly, running forward and holding up his shield to show the king.

"Well done! I knew you could do it!" King Arthur said. He gave them both a warm smile. "Kneel before me, young Knights of Right. Your training is going well. You have earned your first piece of armor. Tell me, what enemy did you face?"

"Hey, that's weird!" Ben said. "We never had to fight any enemy!"

"Are you sure?" King Arthur smiled.

"Well, Ben didn't inhale paint fumes, and I

didn't take pills, so maybe the enemy was stuff that's bad for you?" Joseph guessed.

"Wow, that was deep, Joseph," Ben joked. Joseph stuck his tongue out at his brother.

"You are on the right track, Joseph. The enemy you faced was drugs. Protecting your minds against the evils of drugs will help you think clearly and remain strong. These are important traits in a Knight of the Round Table."

King Arthur placed a hand on each boy's head. "You have shown great courage under pressure. I am proud of you for learning to defend yourselves. Do you remember the story I told you about the Two-Headed Snake?" Both boys nodded as Arthur sat back down on his throne.

"He considered himself so powerful that he needed no defense. He carried two swords, which meant he had no arm free to carry a shield of protection. Drugs are one of the deadly darts that you must face. Remember to defend yourselves at all times. This is the first step to becoming great knights."

"We'll remember," Ben and Joseph promised.

"Where is the Black Knight now?" Ben asked.

"The Black Knight is dangerous, but he is not all-powerful. He was not aware that you had entered the woods. With luck you will be able to return home without drawing his attention. You are safe at home, for the knight

is bound to the forest, and he cannot follow you past the last trees. But be careful when you are in the woods. The Black Knight waits for my power to be weakened so he can destroy me and all who come to my aid," King Arthur warned.

Joseph and Ben nodded.

King Arthur motioned for them to stand. "I must not detain you any longer. The falcon will guide you as you prepare for your next enemy. He will bring you here when the time is right for further instruction. Remember that the shield of True Heart will always protect you."

"Thanks, Your Highness!" Joseph called as they headed for the door.

"See you later, Your Majesty!" Ben yelled back.

"Right makes might, my boys. Right makes might," King Arthur called after them.

10

THE THIRD KNIGHT

The boys hadn't traveled very far when True Heart gave a warning shriek, and the Black Knight swung down from a branch that hung over the path ahead of them. He landed so heavily the ground shook. He raised his crossbow to eye level.

"We aren't going to make it!" Ben shouted.

"Quick! Your shield!" Joseph yelled. They ran, swerving through the trees with their shields raised in front of them. True Heart dived and pecked at the Black Knight, preventing him from taking aim. The boys didn't let down their shields. Even when they were past the knight, they ran backwards as fast as they could to keep their shields between them and the crossbow. When they were almost to the last stand of trees, Joseph tripped over a log and fell to the ground.

"Ben!" he yelled. "Help me!"

Ben stood in front of his brother with his shield raised. There was a hard thump as an arrow hit Ben's shield, but it fell broken and harmless to the ground.

"Awesome!" Ben shouted. "I love my shield!"

Joseph staggered to his feet, holding a plant in his hand. Together they raced the last few feet to the clearing. Ben looked back to

see the Black Knight turning back into the dark woods with True Heart swooping down behind him.

"You aren't so tough, Black Knight!" Ben yelled. "Just wait! One day I'm going to fight you."

Joseph tugged at the back of his brother's shirt and dragged him toward the fence at the edge of their yard.

As they climbed over the fence, they saw Dad lighting a fire in the barbeque grill.

"Hey, boys! There you are. We're having a barbeque tonight and we invited Sam and her family. Is that okay with you?" Dad called.

"Sure, that's great, Dad!" Joseph gave his dad a thumbs-up. Dad smiled, closed the lid of the grill, and went back inside.

"Phew! That was a close one," Joseph said as they climbed the ladder to the tree house. "Ben, isn't this the same kind of plant that T. H. wouldn't let you take out of his beak?"

"Yeah, I think so. Where did you get it?" Ben asked.

"When I fell in the woods, I landed in a patch of this stuff, and I remembered that it might have been a clue."

Ben picked up the strange plant. "Now that the quest is over, let's try to figure out what T. H. was trying to tell us. The first clue was the skull and crossbones. It didn't have anything to do with pirates. But a skull and crossbones also stands for poison. I know the stuff Duke and his friends were sniffing was poison to their bodies."

"That's true," Joseph reflected. "And the doctor's kit makes sense because prescription pills are drugs. Bad people can make something deadly out of medicine that's supposed to help you."

"But what's this thing?" Ben asked, holding up the plant.

"I know some drugs are made from plants. I bet this is a drug too, and that's why T. H.

didn't want us to have it. I shouldn't have picked it, but now how can we get rid of it?" Joseph scratched his head.

"We can't just leave it in the backyard—and someone might find it if we throw it in the trash." Ben frowned. "The grill! We could burn it up in the grill!"

The boys quickly climbed down the tree and ran over to the grill. Joseph opened it up, and Ben tossed the plant into the flames.

Just then Sam came out carrying a salad and saw them burning the plant.

"Oh, my gosh! What are you doing?" she asked, horrified. She threw the salad bowl on the table. Then she grabbed the plant with salad tongs and threw it on the ground.

"We were burning this plant we found. We think it's bad," Joseph explained.

"Yeah, it is—really bad. That's marijuana. People smoke it. Starting it on fire was about the worst thing you could do! Where in the world did you get this?" Sam demanded.

Joseph stammered something about the woods.

"Uh, Sam," Ben interrupted, "maybe we could have the lecture later. The plant is still burning, and it's started the grass on fire!"

"Oh, no!" Sam yelled. She covered her mouth and nose with the sleeve of her jacket to keep from breathing the smoke from the drug. Joseph and Ben covered their mouths, too.

Sam took off her jacket and raised it to

start beating the flames. As the jacket came down to the ground, there was a loud snap. The jacket didn't hit the fire; instead, it hit a shield. A third falcon shield had smothered the flames underneath it.

"Oh, my gosh!" Sam exclaimed. "Where did that come from?"

The boys looked at the shield in shock. "No way! You're the girl King Arthur was talking about!" Joseph cried in surprise.

"Our babysitter is a knight, too? Cool!" Ben shouted.

"What are you two talking about?" Sam choked, waving at the smoke in the air.

"Have you heard anything about the Knights of the Round Table?" Joseph asked as they dragged Sam to the tree house.

"Can girls be knights?" Ben asked before she could answer.

"King Arthur would sure hear it from me if they couldn't," said Sam.

"That's just what I was thinking," Joseph laughed.

"Welcome to the club," Ben said as he laughed with his brother.

Okay, Knights of Right, let's see if you've earned your armor. King Arthur has a few questions for you . . .

1. Why is it important to say no to drugs?

2. What would you have done if you had been with Ben in the garage and your friends wanted you to sniff something harmful?

3. What would you have done if you had been with Joseph in the tent and your friends offered you some pills?

4. When is it okay to use prescription drugs?

5. Why do some kids give in to peer pressure and try drugs?

6. Have you seen or heard about drugs at school? Do you know anyone who has tried drugs?

7. Do you think Samantha (Sam) is a good example for the boys? Why?

8. What do you plan to do if someone offers you drugs?

King Arthur asks—Did you know?

1. Prescription painkillers, when taken inappropriately, can cause addiction. They affect the same areas of the brain as heroin (National Institute on Drug Abuse, "Increased Abuse of Prescription Drugs Is Cause for Concern," 2007; available at http://www.nida.nih.gov/about/welcome/message304.html).

2. Inhalants can kill you the very first time you use them (U.S. Department of Health and Human Services, Substance Abuse and Mental Health Services Administration, "Tips for Teens: Inhalants," 2002. See http://ncadi.samhsa.gov/govpubs/phd631/).

3. Chronic inhalant abusers may permanently lose the ability to perform such everyday functions as walking, talking, and thinking (ibid).

4. Children become addicted to drugs faster than adults (Partnership for a Drug-Free America, "13 Myths about Drug Abuse & Treatment," http://www.drugfree.org/Intervention/WhereStart/13_Myths_About_Drug_Abuse).

5. Illegal drugs can damage the brain, heart, and other important organs. Cocaine can cause a heart attack even in kids and teens (KidsHealth.org, "What You Need to Know about Drugs," http://kidshealth.org/PageManager.jsp?dn=PrimaryChildrens&article_set=22662&lic=5&cat_id=20185#).

6. Signs that someone is on drugs include acting moody and irritable, wanting to be alone, losing interest in old friends and activities, sleeping a lot, having red or puffy eyes, and having a runny nose all the time (ibid).

**Remember, Knights, right makes might.
Keep making good choices and
earning your armor!**

King Arthur

ABOUT THE AUTHOR

M'Lin Rowley is seventeen years old and attends American Fork High School in Utah, where her mascot is a caveman rather than a knight. She loves snow skiing, rock climbing, going to movies with her friends, and writing stories. M'Lin hopes that people will enjoy her books and learn something from them. *The Falcon Shield*, book 1 of the Knights of Right series, is her debut novel.